The Budgie Said Grrrr!

by Martin Waddell

The Budgie Said Grrrr!

Bill went to the Bird Shop and bought a budgie. It was a nice little budgie with blue and green feathers.

"What shall I feed it on?" Bill asked the man. "Birdseed," said the man.

"Grrrr!" said the budgie, hopping up and down.

Bill took the budgie home and showed it to his mum.

"That's a pretty budgie," said Bill's mum, and she popped it into its cage.

"Grrrr!" said the budgie.

"Dinner time, Budgie," said Bill, and he gave the budgie its dinner.

The budgie wouldn't eat the birdseed. It didn't like birdseed. Instead, it ate the bird-bath and the mirror and its tinkly bell.

"Your budgie's getting bigger, Bill," said Bill's mum.

"Grrrr!" said the budgie, and the bell tinkled softly inside it.

The budgie grew and grew.

"What a big budgie!" cried Mrs Rice from next door, getting too close to the cage. The budgie pulled oft her feather hat, and ate it.

"What an appetite!" said Bill.

"Grrrr!" said the budgie, choking on the feathers.

Bill bought the budgie a new cage because it was getting MUCH bigger.

"Nice new house for Budgie!" said Bill's mum.

"Grrrr!" said the budgie, bending the bars.

"I've got the World Champion Budgie!" Bill boasted, and he took it to school to show everybody. "No pets allowed," cried Mr Sloane.

"Grrrr!" said the budgie.

It ate the PE gear and all the school bags and most of the chalk and Mr Sloane's trousers.

Bill took the budgie home in a taxi, and it ate the spare tyre.

"Who is that in the sitting room, watching the wrestling on TV?" asked Bill's dad, when he came home.

"That's my budgie," said Bill proudly.

"Grrrr!" said the budgie, and it ate the TV set and the aerial and the plug.

The Postman came next morning, and rang the doorbell. The budgie opened the door, rubbing its eyes.

"Good morning! Post!" said the Postman.

"Grrrr!" yawned the budgie, and it ate all his letters and the sack, as a sort of Before-Breakfast Snack. The Postman ran away.

PC Jones came when the budgie was finishing off the Registered Airmail Parcels in the garden. "What's all this then?" said PC Jones.

"Grrrr!" said the budgie, and it ate his notebook and his pencil and his walkie talkie and his whistle.

"Grrrr... *peeeeeep!*" said the budgie as it went back inside.

Bill bought a BIGGER cage for the budgie. But the budgie wouldn't go in. "Grrr-peep!" the budgie said, and it put Bill and Mum and Dad in the cage instead.

The budgie gave Bill's dad a packet of birdseed to have for his dinner.

"I don't like birdseed for dinner!" said Bill's dad. "Neither does my budgie," said Bill.

"I want GOOD FOOD!" said Bill's dad.

So the budgie brought him a bath and a mirror, but it couldn't find a tinkly bell.

"I can't eat baths and mirrors!" said Bill's dad, getting angry.

"Grrr-peep!" agreed the budgie.

"Nice Budgie! Pretty Budgie!" pleaded Bill's mum. "Won't you let us out of our cage?"

"Grrr-peep!" said the budgie.

"Why not? asked Bill.

"Because I'm NOT nice and I'm NOT pretty. I'm a Budgie*grrrr*, see?" said the budgie. And it wrote

BUDGIEGRRRRRR RULES - OK?

in left-over birdseed on the floor.

"Why do you go 'Grrrr' all the time, Budgie?" Bill asked.

"You'd go 'Grrrr' all the time if you'd been eating bird-baths and mirrors and tinkly bells and feather hats and PE gear and schoolbags and chalk and trousers and spare tyres and TV sets and aerials and plugs and letters and sacks and Registered Airmail Parcels and notebooks and pencils and walkie talkies and... *peep*, pardon me... whistles," said the budgie.

"WHY DON'T YOU EAT BIRDSEED?" shouted Bill's mum, and Bill's dad, and Bill, all together.

"I don't peep like it," said the budgie. "**Grrrrrrrrrrrr!**"

"If you let me out, I'll make you something good to eat," said Bill's mum, and the budgie let her out.

She made:

apple-fruitcake

ice-cream

shortbread

fish cakes

toffee apples

nut cracknel

strawberry jelly

chips

pizza

hamburgers

sausages

raspberries

beans

honey buns

chocolate mousse

and asparagus

The budgie ate everything - except the asparagus. "Mmmmmmmmmmmmmm!" it said.

"Now THAT's what budgies REALLY like!"

And Bill and Bill's mum and Bill's dad all lived happily ever after with the Biggest Best Fed Budgie in the World (who never said Grrrr! anymore.)

Our Headmaster

Our Headmaster, awful fat
Wind blew off Headmaster's hat
Blew it under a steamroller
Headmaster chased blown-off
bowler.

Bowler bowled, roller rolled,
Imagine that,
Headmaster... FLAT!

Big Bad Bertie

Bertie Simcocks was a funny baby. He smoked a pipe and drank beer and played cards all day long in his pram. When he wasn't drinking and smoking and playing cards, he sang noisy songs.

"Who's that singing noisy songs?" the neighbours complained.

Mrs Simcocks beamed and said, "It's my Bertie."

Auntie Beatie said "That boy will come to no good."

When Bertie Simcocks was four, he stole an elephant. He went to Nursery School on it, and the elephant sat on little Miss Watts, the teacher with the glasses.

"Who's that sitting on the elephant that is sitting on Miss Watts?" asked all the children.

Mrs Simcocks said, "That's my Bertie. He has a way with animals."

Auntie Beatie didn't say a thing.

Bertie Simcocks had to go to school when he was five, but he didn't take his elephant. Instead, he zoomed to school on a rocket, and crashed right through the wall of the classroom.

"Who's been knocking down my classroom?" asked the teacher.

Mrs Simcocks said, "Didn't Bertie do well, zooming through all that traffic?"

Auntie Beatie was very cross with Bertie.

Uncle Albert gave Bertie Simcocks a bulldozer for his eleventh birthday. It was a big bulldozer, with fifteen gears. Bertie drove straight down to town, through all the houses, and bulldozed the Town Hall.

"Who did that?" gasped the mayor, choking on the dust.

"My Bertie's no dozer," said Mrs Simcocks, and she took Bertie home on the bus.

After Bertie Simcocks left school, he made a lot of money robbing banks. He sent some home to his mum and spent the rest on himself.

"Who's that driving past in the Rolls-Royce?" people asked.

And Mrs Simcocks said, "That's my boy, Bertie, God bless him!"

Auntie Beatie waved, but Bertie didn't wave back.

The police heard about Bertie Simcocks. They tried to lock him up, but Bertie bought all the prisons and turned them into luxury holiday camps, with heated swimming pools in each room.

He had sixteen wives, all at the same time - and a camel. "Who is that with sixteen wives and a camel?" all the people asked.

"That's Bertie," said Mrs Simcocks proudly. "Well I never did," said Auntie Beatie with a sniff.

Bertie used some of his money for the people. He built **The Bertie Simcocks Leisure Centres** and **The Bertie Simcocks Funfairs** and he gave away free fish and chips.

Bertie Simcocks was made King, and the bells rang out all over the countryside.

"Who is our favourite King?" shouted everyone.

"My Bertie is," said Mrs Simcocks. Auntie Beatie put:

By Appointment to King Bertie

on her whelk stall.

Then, one day, Mrs Simcocks died. Bertie was very upset.

"You'll miss her now she's gone," said Auntie Beatie. And Bertie cried.

After that, things didn't go so well for Bertie. He got fed up with robbing banks - most of which he owned himself. He got fed up with being rich, so he gave all his money away.

He quarrelled with his wives and they left him.

"I shouldn't have done all those bad things. I don't deserve to be King," Bertie told his sad camel. "I'm going home now. This is goodbye."

Bertie's camel went back to the desert and Bertie headed for home... but he had no home to go to. Mrs Simcocks' little house had been turned into a supermarket.

"Who's that living in a tent behind the baked beans?" asked the customers. But no-one knew.

When Bertie Simcocks was fifty-seven, he was run over by a steam roller, and absolutely flattened.

"I always said he'd come to a sticky end," said Auntie Beatie. "Bertie was no good." But then, she had never loved him.

A very FLAT Bertie Simcocks went up to Heaven.

"Who is that very flat person sitting on a cloud?" somebody said.

"It's my Bertie!" said Mrs Simcocks.

"I'm sorry I was so bad, Mum," Bertie said.

"That's good to hear, Bertie dear," said Mrs Simcocks.

And she gave her flat Bertie a big hug - taking care not to let him slip through her arms!